S0-AAB-574

Gail Wells

Cover by: Antonio Gravante, Jose Resendez, and Gail Wells

For You
And
Everyone else

It's never too late to be what you might have been.

~ George Eliot

Do you believe in Wishes?

Some say, *yes, w*hile others might say, *no.*

I happen to think that wishes are like wind or gravity. You can't actually see wind or gravity,

but you know the effect that it has on you and those around you.

The same goes for wishes.

CHAPTER 1

HOME IS WHERE THE STORY BEGINS

I have the best view from where I live.

Little did I know that I would actually be involved in Mary Iris' life one day.

It was years ago and……

Mary Iris' mother and father had died when she was just a baby. She had no other family. But Yulianna, who was a dear friend and neighbor, took Mary Iris in and raised her as her own. Yulianna never married and had no children of her own. She grew up in Guatemala, of Mayan ancestry, and brought many of her beliefs and traditions with her when she left her country. Yulianna was the first of her family to live outside the highlands of Guatemala. It was Mary Iris' mother, Claire, who had taught Yulianna how to speak English. Yulianna wished with all her might, that she would be able to raise Mary Iris to be a happy child. She hoped that she would be able to teach her that we are all born with a special gift that helps us fulfill our purpose in life. At least, that's what Yulianna's parents taught her. As Yulianna held Mary Iris in her arms, she thought about what Mary Iris should call her. It couldn't be Madre, Mami, Mom, Mother, and certainly not Aunt or Auntie. "It's just *you and me*, Mary Iris," Yulianna said as she looked at her tenderly. And… with that it came to her. "*You and me…. Tú y yo. LO TENGO!*" she shouted, which startled Mary Iris.

"I will take the *Yu* from my name, and the *M* and *I* for Mary Iris. Mi pequeño, to you… I will be Yumi." Yulianna spoke softly this time as she gently rocked Mary Iris in her arms. With that the little baby smiled at Yulianna.

Even from where I was, I could feel the love

between the two of them.

As Mary Iris grew older I noticed how she loved to dance and I watched Yumi teach her how to garden in the Mayan ways.   The little family grew flowers with the most beautiful blooms, and fruits and vegetables that provided them with the most wonderful of meals.

I would hear Yumi say to Mary Iris, "A seed... has everything inside it to be exactly what it's supposed to be. Corn will never be anything other than corn and an acorn will become an oak tree that will give us shade, food for the animals and it makes our air better to breathe." Then she would go on saying, "This of course... will only happen if the seed is nourished.   It's the same for humans... and nourishment is more than just food," Yumi said as she hugged Mary Iris then giving her a tickle and a kiss. "You must remember that always Mary Iris."

I loved watching Mary Iris and Yumi. I

learned a lot from them.

One day when Yumi was tending to her stingless bees and Mary Iris was watering the sunflowers, I saw them doing the waggle dance. Now, just in case you don't know what the waggle dance is, it's the dance the bees do to tell each other where there's food to make honey.   It's how the bees talk to each other. The bees buzz as they move around in a figure eight, doing a little waggle in the middle when they change directions.   Mary Iris learned this dance from Yumi, and I loved how it made Mary Iris smile. It's a shame, but I don't think most people think of bees dancing.

Anyway, all of a sudden, Mary Iris noticed a rainbow through the stream of water and asked Yumi, "How does it happen that I can see a rainbow through the water?"

Yumi replied by saying… "Is a miracle!"

Mary Iris continued by asking, "How do the sunflowers know how to follow the sun?"

And once again Yumi replied with, "Is a miracle!"

Just then Mary Iris heard the neighbors baby crying and asked Yumi, "Why do babies cry?"

"Is a miracle." Yumi smiled as she looked up to the heavens. "There are miracles all around us every day. Most people take them for granted. I was taught to never take for granted even the smallest of miracles." Yumi said as she continued tending to her bees.

Mary Iris dipped her finger into the sweet honey that Yumi had just extracted from the honeycomb and knew that this too was a miracle. This of course made Mary Iris even more aware of miracles, so she started to make a list of them in a journal which she titled…

My List of Miracles

1. *Rainbows and how the colors are always in the same order.*
2. *Skunks and how they're peaceful creatures but let off a bad smell.*
3. *Lemon trees have sweet smelling flowers, but lemons are reeeealllllly sour.*
4. *I think it's a miracle that the hair on our head grows and grows, but not the hair on our eyebrows or arms.*

Needless to say, this made me think more

about miracles.

I especially enjoyed watching Yumi and Mary Iris at Christmas. Yumi had learned Mary Iris' mothers' Christmas traditions, and Yumi was happy to be able to pass them on to Mary Iris. Her most favorite was the special gingerbread cookie recipe. Yumi remembered Mary Iris' mother telling her, that the recipe had been passed down from her mother, which of course would be Mary Iris' grandmother. They would also make Yumi's special Christmas tamales. It was not a written recipe but a process made with love that was passed down from generation to generation. To me, tamales always looked like little presents and I wondered if that was why they were made at Christmas?

Yumi also taught Mary Iris that people all over the world have their own traditions and celebrate in different ways and sometimes on different days, but all for the same meaning. "This is a time to celebrate the light of the world," Yumi would say. Yumi told Mary Iris about Christmas in Guatemala and how it's celebrated with fireworks. She also told her about the special rooster ornament that was always last to be hung on the Christmas tree.

"An old legend says that a rooster crowed at the stroke of midnight on Christmas Eve when baby Jesus was born. Was a miracle, Mary Iris!   In Guatemala, we have a Misa de Gallo. A rooster's mass."   With that said; Yumi and Mary Iris put on some music and danced around and crowed like roosters. It was quite the sight.

After their dance was done, Yumi thought it might be a good time to tell Mary Iris about *The Magic List*. "Mary Iris...   did you know that Santa not only has a list of good boys and girls, he has a Magic List? This list is much smaller than the list of good boys and girls and not for young children.   You see, to get on the list you must do everything you can to make the world a better place, and of course you must always believe in Santa. Then... you have to make a wish!   Sometimes when people get older, they have a hard time believing.   Believing that they can make the world a better place, believing in Santa, believing in wishes. Sometimes they don't even believe in themselves," Yumi said shaking her head in despair. "Follow me," she said.

Mary Iris followed Yumi into Yumi's bedroom. Yumi opened the top drawer of her dresser and pulled out an envelope to show Mary Iris. Inside the envelope was a certificate that had been awarded to "Yulianna" as an honorary member of Santa's Magic List. At the bottom of the certificate was Santa Claus' signature.

"I've never stopped believing, not even for one minute," Yumi explained. "My parents and I would leave on Christmas Eve to go into town to see the fireworks. On our way we would make our Christmas wish. After the fireworks we would go to church for the Misa de Gallo and when we came back home, there would be fruits and candies from Santa. In Guatemala, we call him Papa Noel. Mami and Papi could not afford such wonderful treats, so it was truly a special gift we all enjoyed. It made our Christmas very special, and oh, they were so delicious. You know what Mary Iris? Papa Noel still brings my parents fruits and candies every year."

Yumi went on to tell Mary Iris that when she was a young girl, she wished that she could help her parents so they wouldn't have to work so hard. At the same time, Yulianna's parents wished for a better life for Yulianna. She also told Mary Iris that when she was 32, a woman by the name of Coralee came to the village where she lived.

"Coralee was looking for one person to whom she could offer a scholarship at an American University. Everyone in the village thought she would pick somebody young. She spoke with many teens who were interested in going to America. They all wanted to make better lives for themselves. But I was very lucky and Coralee chose me," Yumi said feeling very proud.

Yulianna not only wanted a better life for herself and her parents, but she hoped that she could help to show people that while new ideas and ways of living are very important, the ancestors' ways should not be forgotten.

"El pasado nos hace ser lo que somos hoy en dia.   Me siento orgulloso de ser de Guatemala y Maya.   Pero la major raza es la raza humana. He deseado esto por muchos anos, I told Coralee, which means…, The past makes us who we are today.   I am proud to be from Guatemala, and Mayan.   But, the best race, is the human race," Yumi said as Mary Iris listened.   "I told her that I had wished for this for many years."

Coralee was touched that Yulianna had never given up on her dream and was impressed that Yulianna spoke Spanish along with her native Quiché language.   Not long after their meeting, Yulianna was on her way to America. Her parents were happy for her, as their wish for Yulianna to have a better life was coming true.

After Yulianna arrived in America, she met Claire, who tutored English to students from Latin America.   Yulianna and Claire became best of friends and Yulianna eventually moved next door to Claire.   Yulianna was Claire's maid of honor at her wedding, and was at the hospital the day that Mary Iris was born.   And the rest as they say; is history. Coralee and Yulianna still keep in touch from time to time by way of letter writing and sometimes a phone call.   Coralee now calls Yulianna, Yumi, just like Mary Iris does.   She thinks the name suits her perfectly.

*I happen to think
it suits her perfectly as well.*

CHAPTER 2

LET ME INTRODUCE MYSELF

Now, before I go on, I suppose I should properly introduce myself to you.   My name is Will. I'm a star!   Not a movie star, not a TV star, and certainly not a rock star. Not in the way you would think anyway.   I'm a star – you know, of the twinkling kind.   I come from the Galaxy of Dreamers, not so far away.   My name is Will, because when people wish on me, their wish "*will*" come true and I… have "*WILLL*" power, (no pun intended.)   When you look up at the night sky, I'm white.   That's what people see, but actually, I'm many different colors. A bit unusual for us stars – but to the human eye, what you see, is white.   I help to orchestrate and choreograph the rhythm of the night sky and I… have magical powers.   My friends call me a *White Rhythmic Wizard* which is one reason why it didn't surprise me that Mary Iris came into my life. We both love, love, love to dance!

If you were to look up at the night sky and you see a star that's really twinkling and moving about, but not like a shooting star – I'll tell you about shooting stars later – well , that would most likely be me. Dancing to the rhythm of the universe.   I'm not the biggest star by any means, or even one of the most well-known stars.   Actually, I'm pretty much a nobody as far as stars go. But, I know my place in space.   My home.   Us stars, well, we don't move around too much.   Except for dancing, twinkling, and shooting, or if we're on a wish granting mission, we don't move out of place with each other.   We can't. It would disrupt the natural way of the universe.   It's called *Proper Motion.*   We made this decision a very, very, long time ago.   As long as there have been humans, they've used us for celestial navigation. That is why it's imperative that we have *Proper Motion.*

Now, let me tell you what I see when I look at Earth.   I see lights.   Much like when you look at us stars.   I don't see lights made by what you call electricity, batteries, candlelight, or solar-powered light. Not even the light by fire.   No, I see the lights of the human spirit.   The Earth hasn't been very bright lately.   Us stars, we decided to work together to teach people about what we call *heart wishes.* They're the kind of wishes that will help to raise the Earth's brightness.   You see, one of the problems we've encountered are the NCF's, aka, the Naysayer Cosmic Force.   They're the troublemakers of the worst kind, and one of the reasons why my galaxy has yet to officially been discovered.   The Naysayers on Earth say it doesn't exist.   If that were true, that would mean, I don't exist and if I don't exist, how could I ever tell this story????

Anyway, the NCF's, they disguise themselves as stars.   Bright shining imposters that have a vortex so strong, they will suck you in without you even knowing it.   The people that make their wishes on these star imposters, well, their wishes go kaplooey. And that my friends, is the reason why the Earth's brightness is fading.   People have been making the wrong kinds of wishes on these star imposters and then they themselves become Naysayer's.   My friends and I have been working on some ideas about how to resolve this atrocity.

A good friend of mine by the name of Kapteyn, decided that it was time to put those ideas to good use and teach people about *heart wishes.*   He told us that *heart wishes* are stronger than any vortex caused by the NCF's.   We were all happy to hear that. So, there we were, just waiting for that special moment, that we may have the privilege to be wished on by someone with a *heart wish.*   Well, it happened to me.   Not just one wish, but two!!!   At the same time!!!!!   It was synergy, serendipity, a fortuitous happenstance… it was – a *Miracle!*

I'll never forget it!

CHAPTER 3

TWO WISH ON A STAR

It was what people on Earth call November. This is very confusing to me since the word *November* came from the Latin word *novem*, which means nine and November used to be the ninth month. Now, it's the eleventh month because the humans decided to change the calendar.

Sorry, all that's beside the point, o.k. back to the story.

One fateful night, on a November's full moon many years ago, two people made a wish – on me – at the exact same time. It was Mary Iris who was seven at the time and, a boy by the name of Chris. I couldn't believe it. Out of all the billions and billions of stars in the sky, Mary Iris picked me. Who would have ever thought that another person would pick me at the very same time? I'm not a mathematical wizard, but chances are slim to none that something like this would ever happen. I have to say, those wishes rocked my world. I had finally gotten my calling, twofold.

Mary Iris wished to spread happiness while teaching dances from around the world and also that someday she too might be on Santa's Magic List. Chris, well, he wished to be a pilot some day and help people who were hit by natural disasters.   You see, Chris' parents had been on a vacation in a faraway land when an earthquake had struck, never to return home.   Because of this, Chris lived with his grandma. He also wished that someday his grandma might see him raise his own family.

Well I knew this was all going to be very interesting.   I had seen Santa and his reindeer from my galaxy, but experiencing this Christmas thing, was going to be new to me.   Actually, this Earthly experience was going to be new.   I figured all I had to do was find Santa.   He's good at fulfilling wishes and I'd ask him to consider putting Mary Iris on his Magic List.   It's funny, 'cause as I started thinking about fulfilling Mary Iris and Chris' wishes... I found that I was making a wish of my own.   My wish was that when people would hear this story, it might just help cut down on that nasty energy of the Naysayer Cosmic Force, and... more people would start believing again, and... the Earth would be brighter, and... it would give us stars more to look at!   And ... I would do a happy dance!!!!

Well, unfortunately, most people don't know how to wish.   They think their wishes should come true right away.   They don't realize that wishes don't get granted on the spot.   The granting of wishes is not set by what you call a clock, and you can't mark it on a calendar.   No siree.   It goes by the time of the universe. It's what's called *natural time*.   *Natural time* isn't a time of day or a date on a calendar. *Natural time* is like when the sun rises or sets. Flowers bloom in the time of their clock, spring and summer, and the snow falls in winter.   This could be

January in some places, and August in others. When you're tired, your body says it's time to rest, so you sleep. All of those things are *natural time*.

Now, remember what I said about heart wishes??? A heart wish will not only benefit the wisher, but the rest of the world, be it big or small. I contacted my friend Kapteyn to let him know what had happened and that I was ready, willing and able to fulfill these wishes. He promised to help me out in any way that he could.

What I have yet to tell you, is that there is a legend of the universe, almost as old as time itself, that says each star carries the soul of one person. The ancients believed this, and we stars know it to be true. When a connection is made between the human soul and the star soul, these soul mates help each other to shine even brighter. Most of the time these soul mates aren't even aware that this is happening. In case you couldn't guess it already, Mary Iris is my soul mate. I thank my lucky stars that this happened so perfectly. It was serendipitous! I was going to meet Mary Iris. Well… kind of. We stars can't actually meet humans face to face, so we change our star form into a human form when needed. I left immediately. Off I was from the *Galaxy of Dreamers*, (eleven light years away), to Earth. Mary Iris and Chris were going to have their wishes come true. I was going to see to that! As I travelled those eleven light years, I continued to watch Mary Iris, and from time to time I would also check in on Chris.

I'm hoping you want to hear more.

CHAPTER 4

MARY IRIS' BEST FRIEND

The summer Mary Iris was nine years old and I had already been traveling for 2 years, Yumi and Mary Iris got a puppy.   The puppy was black as night except for one small marking on her chest and her fur was thick and fluffy. I must say for all the puppies I've seen as I look upon the Earth, she was as big or bigger than most dogs are when they're fully grown. They named her *Shambahla.* An unusual name I must say, but apparently Mary Iris' mother would play a song about a utopian place called Shambahla. It was a happy song and one of the first songs Yumi learned in English. Yumi thought that it might just be the perfect name for the new addition to their family and Mary Iris agreed.

Once when Mary Iris was walking Shambahla, Shambahla saw another dog that she wanted to play with. Off she went, not knowing her own strength, pulling Mary Iris to the ground, skinning her arms and legs.   Mary Iris yelled to Shambahla to stop… and she did.   That was when Mary Iris decided to teach Shambahla how to listen and be respectful.

"Shambahla," Mary Iris said as she looked her in the eyes. "You are big and strong, and you hurt me." Shambahla hung her head low and gave Mary Iris those sad puppy eyes as if to say "sorry." Mary Iris went on to say "Not all dogs are friendly like you, so we need to walk up to them with caution. Let's be more careful next time, o.k. girl?" With that Shambahla gave Mary Iris a big sloppy kiss, which made Mary Iris giggle as she wiped the slobber from her face.

They were the best of friends. Mary Iris would tell Shambahla everything… all of her dreams, thoughts and wishes. They spent all their free time together. When Mary Iris was out in the garden, Shambahla was right by her side. Shambahla especially loved to drink the cold water from the hose as Mary Iris watered the garden. Sometimes Mary Iris would spray the water over her head and Shambahla would shake it off, as the water – and her drool – would fly all over the place getting Mary Iris wet and slimy.

When Mary Iris would dance, Shambahla would watch closely. Sometimes she would dance along with Mary Iris and it was then that I noticed that dogs can also smile. When the day would be done and Mary Iris would call it a night, Shambahla laid on the floor next to her bed. After Mary Iris would go to sleep, Shambahla would sneak into her bed. Of course Shambahla only thought she was sneaking, because for a dog her size it would be safe to say that it would go unnoticed. Mary Iris would open her sleepy eyes, pat Shambahla on her head and say "go to sleep girl," and the two of them would sleep side by side until morning.

Sometimes I would watch as Yumi and Mary Iris would have pancakes for breakfast. Yumi would make an extra one just for Shambahla. She wasn't allowed to have it until they had finished theirs. They would tell her to go into the other room and she did. She waited patiently for them to say "O.K., it's your turn." And when they did, she would come running into the kitchen wagging her tail with drool profusely coming from her mouth in the anticipation of what she was about receive. Mary Iris would say, "Sit" and Shambahla would sit as she would get her first piece of pancake. Then Mary Iris would say "speak," as she got another piece and then, Shambahla would do trick after trick until the pancake was gone. I've never seen such a smart dog.

I was looking forward to meeting Shambahla. Where I come from, the only dog we have, is Sirius. Sirius is the brightest star in the night sky that can be seen from Earth and sometimes is called the *Big Dog Star*. Sirius has a companion called Sirius B. Mary Iris' companion is called Shambahla. I think it's nice to have a companion.

As I continued on my journey, Yumi continued to teach Mary Iris about life. She taught Mary Iris to believe in her uniqueness and told her about a special light that's inside us all – our own special gift that helps to make the rest of the world shine.

"Not only do we have teachers at school, but we learn lessons daily from life itself," Yumi explained. "You can even learn lessons from Shambahla --- like how she's always happy to see you, and how to live in the here and now." Yumi taught Mary Iris about people and how they're alike and different and to honor and respect all people and their differences.   "There are good things that happen to people in life and sometimes not so good things," said Yumi.   "Always know that after the rain, there is a rainbow."

I love rainbows, but did you know there are

also moonbows?

CHAPTER 5

WHAT'S IN A NAME?

As I continued on with my journey, a few more Earthly years had passed. It was getting close to Christmas. Mary Iris was now in the sixth grade.   I was checking in on Mary Iris at school one day and noticed that some of Mary Iris' classmates were making fun of her because Mary Iris told them that she still believed in Santa Claus.   This was just about the time I was crossing the path of a Naysayer Cosmic Force, so I thought that maybe because I was crossing this path, it might be the reason why all this was happening. I saw a girl named Agnes who was also laughing, which surprised Mary Iris because although she didn't know Agnes very well, she never seemed to be the kind of person that would be mean. Agnes, along with the others told Mary Iris that she must be nuts for still believing in Santa Claus.

"A mighty oak was once a nut and I'm a mighty oak," Mary Iris stated firmly with her hands on her hips.

This made her classmates laugh even harder. I think what Mary Iris really meant was that she held her beliefs strongly and she wasn't going to change them just because someone didn't agree with her.   It reminded me of a quote I had heard once by a man named *John Eliot.* He said; "History shows us that the people who end up changing the world – the great political, social, scientific, technological, artistic, even sports revolutionaries – are always nuts, until they are right, and then they are geniuses."   If you ask me, I think Mary Iris was a genius for standing up to them. Luckily for me, I was able to pass through the Naysayer Cosmic Force with just a bit of turbulence.

When Mary Iris got home from school that day, she talked to Yumi about what had happened.

"Sometimes people do this because it makes them feel good – like they have power," Yumi explained.   "They just need to learn how to feel good about themselves in a different way and use that power in a positive way."

"You mean like when I dance?" Mary Iris asked.   "I feel very powerful when I dance."

"Yes, Mary Iris, just like when you dance."

Mary Iris told Yumi about Agnes too. She said; "You know, I never thought she'd be mean, but she was laughing with everyone else."

Yumi sighed remembering what it was like to be Mayan in Guatemala.   "I remember a time like that when I was about your age.   It has been my experience that she probably just wants to fit in, so she goes along with the crowd.   It's hard sometimes when people have different beliefs than you do," Yumi said. It still hurt Mary Iris to be made fun of, but she understood what Yumi was trying to tell her.

The next day at school, Mary Iris approached Agnes and asked why she was being so mean?   Agnes saw that the other kids were watching her as she talked to Mary Iris and said; "You're too old to believe in Santa," as she looked onwards at her classmates.   After her classmates smiled with approval by that remark, they walked away and it was then that Agnes apologized to Mary Iris.

"I've always believed in Santa too," Agnes said. "But, a few years ago, my brothers told me he wasn't real.   I didn't want to be made fun of, so... I said I didn't believe anymore either.   I wanted to keep believing. Deep down I do believe, but they already make enough fun of me because I like poetry. They think it's stupid and not cool, so I try to fit in any way I can.   I'm really sorry.   I wish I could be strong like you."

"I like poetry Agnes.   Can I read some of your poems?" Mary Iris asked. Agnes smiled as she pulled a folder from her backpack handing it to Mary Iris. After reading a few of her poems, Mary Iris told Agnes that she really liked them. Mary Iris confided on how much she loves to dance.   They would get together at each other's houses. Agnes sharing her poetry, and Mary Iris sharing dance.   And... with their friendship, the Earth got a little brighter.

I liked Agnes' poems too and thought that I'd

share a couple of them with you....

The Poetry Writer

Writing is my silent voice,
the paper is the ear.
The pencil doesn't have a choice,
what the mind might fear.

Maybe I should say my words out loud,
maybe all across the nation.
For if I keep them to myself,
It might be
Floccinaucinihilipilification.

The 6th Graders Vocabulary Spoken

Word

This paraphrasing parody,
exploits extracts humanity
hoax to coax and collaborate,
this painstaking calamity.
Ignite esteem, defend respect,
clarity's a rarity.
Liberate, cultivate,
Our unique diversity!

I think that Agnes truly has a gift for writing poetry and I found it very interesting to learn that *floccinaucinihilipilification* is the longest English non medical word that means; *worthless or having little value.* I like to think of it as an oxymoron.

Latter that day as Yumi was talking with Mary Iris she said; "Words are very powerful. They can hurt people like a knife or being hit. But, they can also empower people and make them strong – strong in mind and strong in spirit. Wondrous things can happen if the right words are used. Remember when your classmates said we were weird??? The word *weird* can sometimes be thought of as a negative word because it means *unusual.* But, another way of thinking about it is that it could mean *unique.* You, Mary Iris are unique."

As Yumi gently held Mary Iris' cheeks in her palms she went on to say; "All my life I've heard people be made fun of or ridiculed because of their names, their beliefs, or the color of their skin.   It's very sad.   We are not our names; we are humans. We are all different, yet very much the same.   You my child are one who dances and one who understands. I see you dance when you're happy and when you're sad.   I see you dancing in the garden with Shambahla and with life itself.   I see how you understand people and life.   I was told by a friend of mine years ago that your name should be *Binah.   Binah* is an African name that means *one who dances.*   It's also part of the tree of life and means *understanding.*   I think from now on, just between you and me, I shall call you *Binah."*

It was interesting to me to listen to Yumi talk to Mary Iris about humans and how they are different and the same.   It's the same up here.   We have different kinds of stars and different names for them – giants, supergiants, dwarfs, subdwarfs, red, orange, blue, yellow, and white.   We live in different galaxies, much like your countries on Earth, and different constellations, which are like your states. We are all different, but we are all stars.

Christmas had come and Yumi gave Mary Iris a beautiful music box.   On the top was a painting of a girl dancing with her arms held up to the sky.   When the box was opened, it played the prettiest melody. Inside was a mirror.   When Mary Iris first received the gift, she wound it up, opened the top, and I watched as she and Yumi danced a waltz to the beautiful music.

"This is the most beautiful gift ever!" Mary Iris exclaimed.   "I'll treasure it always," as they continued on with their dance.

"Merry Christmas *Binah,"* Yumi said as they twirled around the room.

In addition to the music box from Yumi, Mary Iris got a book about dances from around the world and some new music from Santa.   Shambahla got a bone and a new leash with stars on it that glow in the dark.   And, as usual, Yumi got her fruits and candies that Santa has been bringing her since she was a little girl.   Later that day, they had Yumi's special Christmas tamales with some friends and of course a plate full of gingerbread cookies.   Eating the gingerbread cookies made Mary Iris think about her mother.   She thought about how grateful she was that her mother had shared the family tradition with Yumi. She hoped that one day she too would share the recipe with her own children.

Names and words are a funny thing. The Sun is anything but a "yellow dwarf," yet that's what you humans classify it as. Floccinaucinihilipilification is such a big word for meaning little value. And, love is a small word in comparison for such a big feeling.

CHAPTER 6

THE NAYSAYER'S REVENGE

Before I knew it Mary Iris was in her high school years. I was travelling at a steady pace and right on schedule. All was well and good until I came upon the Naysayer Cosmic Force once again. They meant business this time and both Mary Iris and I were affected. I started to believe that my journey was a waste of time. Mary Iris had told Mrs. Grey, who was one of her teachers that she wanted to travel the world to learn dances from other countries, and teach people about why we dance. Mrs. Grey told Mary Iris that she'd be wasting her time and said that maybe she should think about something more realistic, like being a nurse or an accountant.

Oh, I was so mad when I heard that. I happen to know that everyone has a special talent and should use it. It isn't that being a nurse or an accountant is a bad thing. It just wasn't in Mary Iris' stars, if you know what I mean. It was after that comment that all of a sudden one of the Naysayer's that looked like a star imposter, spit out a horrendous laugh and told me that Mrs. Grey had wished on him long ago and that was what turned her into a Naysayer. Well, that knocked my senses right back into me. I tried to escape, but the Naysayer Cosmic Force was too strong.   It was like one of those proverbial black holes that you can't get out of.

I happened to notice a small star from not too far away was shooting right towards me. You can only imagine how happy I was. You see, most people think that when they see a shooting star in the sky, that it's one to make a wish on. Not so. A shooting star's too busy to collect wishes. It's one that's on its way to help another star. We see the same thing on Earth; the light of one person helping another person. For her size, I was amazed at her strength. She was able to release me from the NCF faster than the twinkling of a star, which is about the same as a blink of an eye. I was forever grateful!

"How'd you do that?" I asked the tiny star, "You're so small."

"It's not about size," she replied. "It's about the size of the spirit!   It's what makes you feel alive."

I knew what she meant by that. "You're very wise," I said. "What's your name?"

"I don't have a name," the star said. "I'm an orphan star.   I'm not the only one. There are many more like me."

I never really thought about the orphan stars before.   I thanked her for saving me from the Naysayer Cosmic Force and told her that I was on my way to fulfill the wishes of a human girl named Mary Iris and a boy whose name is Chris.

"I hope that someday I too will be wished upon. Bye" she said as she twinkled out of sight.

I realized, thanks to that little star, that this journey was *not* a waste of time and I *would* make it!

And I hoped that the little orphan star with the big spirit might get a name someday.

Unfortunately for Mary Iris, while I was released from the force, she was not. Mrs. Grey had Mary Iris thinking that maybe she wasn't meant to travel the world and learn and teach about dance. Mary Iris had become more quiet and danced less and less as she went about her daily life.

Yumi noticed this and asked Mary Iris why she had been so quiet lately. Mary Iris just shook her head and shrugged her shoulders, telling Yumi that everything was o.k. Yumi couldn't figure it out, but she knew that Mary Iris would come to her if she really needed her help. Even Shambahla had sensed that something was wrong. Of course Mary Iris confided in Shambahla about Mrs. Grey.

In the months that followed, Shambahla stayed by Mary Iris' side. They spent time in the garden together and went for long walks. Shambahla was the only one besides me and Mrs. Grey herself, who knew why Mary Iris doubted herself. Dogs react to peoples' feelings and have a keen sense about negative energy. One day, I noticed when Mary Iris and Shambahla were taking a walk, they passed by Mrs. Grey. Shambahla growled at her, which made Mrs. Grey scared and she started walking faster. This made Mary Iris chuckle inside because that's exactly how she felt about Mrs. Grey, but thought it wouldn't be appropriate if she herself growled at her.

As Mary Iris was getting close to graduating from high school, she told Yumi that she wasn't sure what she wanted to be and thought it might be best if she didn't go to college right away. Yumi allowed her to get a job at the local market knowing that one day Mary Iris would figure it out just like she had. Besides, Shambahla was getting older and Mary Iris wanted to spend as much time as she could with her.

Personally, I think life is hard sometimes and

we question ourselves, but I've found that this is how

we grow.

CHAPTER 7

WHAT ABOUT CHRIS?

I was looking forward to my near arrival on Earth and feeling very excited about Mary Iris and Chris' wishes coming true. I do have to apologize however, because I feel like I've spent so much time telling you about Mary Iris, that I had all but forgotten that you're probably curious about Chris. Unlike Mary Iris, everything for Chris seemed to fall right into place.

Not long after Chris made his wish, he started doing odd jobs at *The Landings*, a small local airport. He would come home telling his grandma stories all about the different planes and the pilots that flew them. He looked forward to the day when he too would be a pilot and have his own stories.

By the time Chris was fourteen, Mr. Avery, Chris' boss and owner of the airport, took Chris under his wing. *Oh, I just make myself laugh sometimes with my choice of words… under his wing – airplanes have wings, get it?* Anyway, Mr. Avery was like a second father to Chris and taught him how to fly. Then, when Chris was sixteen, he not only got his drivers' license, but got his pilot's license as well. This was a cause for a grand celebration, so, Mr. Avery and Chris' grandma got together and threw him a surprise party. Boy oh boy was he ever surprised!

Chris was an excellent student and helped people around town whenever he could. On Sunday afternoons, he would fly his grandma in Mr. Avery's Piper Cub. She enjoyed the time they shared together and was quite proud of the young man Chris had become. *I was too!*

Unlike Mary Iris, Chris never came in contact with a naysayer. After he graduated high school he headed off to college. Four years later, when he graduated college, he set off to do exactly what he had wished. He flew planes to help people in need. His first mission was to fly medical supplies to an area that had been hit by a hurricane.

Chris would always make sure he was home to spend Christmas with his grandma and this year was going to be no different. There was what you might call, one bug in the ointment. A tornado had hit a small town in Oklahoma and left almost the whole town homeless. Chris was there for months helping to rebuild. He was hoping to be back at home with his grandma in time for celebrating, but felt that he needed to stay on to make sure every family was taken care of. Time was running out, so he called his grandma to let her know he couldn't leave just yet but would try his best to be home by Christmas dinner. She told Chris not to worry because she understood the importance of his work.

So there you have it. It was about the time that Chris called his grandma that I entered the Earth's atmosphere. It was good timing and I felt relieved that my mission *was* possible.

I was happy that Chris' wish was coming true without too much effort.   I did wonder however, and I haven't quite figured it out, why it is that some wishes are easier to fulfill than others?

CHAPTER 8

HELLO – GOODBYE

Yumi had gone up North to help Coralee, who had broken her leg and needed some help. She had hoped to be back at home in time for Christmas. Unfortunately, it was taking longer than had been expected. *I was seeing a pattern here. It seemed that both Yumi and Chris might not make it home for their Christmas celebrations.* Mary Iris continued to go to work at the market and was eagerly waiting to hear that Yumi would be back at home in time for Christmas. She missed Yumi and was looking forward to their annual gingerbread cookie baking day.

I made my landing on Earth just as Mary Iris was coming home from work. I watched her in the window as she greeted Shambahla. But there was a problem. The big black dog just laid there, barely able to pick up her head to acknowledge her. Mary Iris ran over to Shambahla and kneeled on the floor next to her. With tears rolling down her face, she petted Shambahla and gently wrapped her arms around her, trying to assure her that everything would be okay. Mary Iris got up and went to the refrigerator for some chicken and fresh water for Shambahla, thinking that this might just perk her up a bit.   But Shambahla just looked at it and laid her big head in Mary Iris' lap.   I watched the two of them all night long. Mary Iris slept on the floor with Shambahla as if she knew it would be her friend's last night.   The next morning, Mary Iris woke up, but Shambahla did not.

"I'm glad we shared so many memories, I'll never forget you," Mary Iris said to her as she wept.

Mary Iris called Yumi to tell her about Shambahla.   Yumi's heart ached that she couldn't be there for Mary Iris.   She too would miss that big old dog and could hardly bear the fact that Mary Iris was there alone.   Just then Yumi had an idea.

"Mary Iris, how about you come up North? We could all spend Christmas together. It's supposed to snow, it would be a new experience for you."

"Maybe a change of scenery might do me some good," Mary Iris replied.

Mary Iris buried Shambahla in the backyard under her favorite shade tree as she sang…*Auld Lang Syne*.   "Good-bye my friend," she said as she went into the house to prepare for her journey the next day. When she finished, she wound the music box that Yumi had given her and danced, missing both Shambahla and Yumi.   As I watched her waltz around her room, I wished that I might share a dance with Mary Iris someday.

Mary Iris cried herself to sleep that night and dreamt about all the good times she shared with her precious canine companion.   She woke up to the sound of Shambahla's bark.   She knew it wasn't real, but thought it was a sign that Shambahla was telling her it was time to leave.

I could tell that Mary Iris' heart was broken. I, too, have lost friends.   They were star friends. And, while they no longer shine in the sky, they sure shine in the memories that I have of them.

CHAPTER 9

THE JOURNEY BEGINS

Mary Iris packed up her car and was on her way. After driving several hours it started to rain.   It started as a gentle rain, then it seemed to be coming down in buckets.   Even though Mary Iris was very careful, the car slid at a curve in the road and Mary Iris got stuck in a rut.   I had wondered if it might be the Naysayer Cosmic Force that caused this.   But something seemed different.   I could see Mary Iris wasn't happy about what had happened, but she knew that everything happens for a reason.   She pulled her rain poncho out of the back seat and started walking hoping to find a town to see if she could get some help.   Not too long after she started on her way the rain stopped. Out came the sun, and Mary Iris noticed a beautiful rainbow.   She smiled as she remembered what Yumi had taught her… *"After the rain, there is a rainbow!"*

Mary Iris continued walking for what seemed like miles and decided to sit under a tree for a while and take a break.   As she sat down on the grass, she noticed a stone with writing on it.   It said; **"Leave no stone unturned."**   Sparking her curiosity, she picked it up and turned it over. The other side said; *"Live the life you imagined."*   "Live the life you imagined, hmmmm," she thought to herself.   "Right now I'm trying to imagine how I'm going to make it to Coralee's in time for Christmas," she said out loud to herself. After her short rest, she was ready to continue on.   "There's got to be a town not too far away," she said as she stood up collecting her backpack brushing the dirt from her pants.

Mary Iris almost took the rock with her, but decided that maybe it needed to stay there for other people to see. As she continued walking, she thought about the message on the rock.   She remembered that there was a time when she was younger when she imagined what she wanted her life to look like and lost it.   But now… since she saw that rock, it was all starting to come back to her.

When she got to the top of a hill, off in the distance she could see a town. As Mary Iris approached the town, she noticed there was a Christmas Market, much like the Christkindlmarkt in Germany.   She stopped at a booth that was selling glass blown ornaments of all different colors and asked a lady if there was anyone in town who had a tow truck.   The lady at the booth told her that the owner of the car repair shop, who owned the only tow truck in town, had left until after Christmas to visit his family.   Mary Iris was pretty tired by this time and asked the lady if there was a local motel?

"Bless your heart child, you won't find a room for miles," she said.   "It's our annual Christmas Gingerbread Festival.   The local bakery makes a life size gingerbread Santa, sleigh, and reindeer.   There's a gingerbread house contest with a special prize given by Santa himself. People come from miles around and all the rooms are filled up months in advance."

Emily Johnson, who owned the local bakery, overheard Mary Iris talking with the lady who was selling the ornaments and offered her house to Mary Iris. Emily was going to be up all night at the bakery with preparations for the big day. Mary Iris gratefully accepted and asked if she might be able to use her phone to call Yumi to let her know what happened. Emily said, "Do whatever you need to do, feel free and make yourself at home."

Mary Iris arrived at Emily's house. It was a charming little cottage across the street from a small lake. The house was decorated for Christmas and in the kitchen was a plate of gingerbread cookies. As she saw the cookies, she longed to be with Yumi. She was once again thinking about how they had missed their annual gingerbread cookie baking day. It was always a special time. Yumi told Mary Iris that the times that people spend together, like baking cookies and making tamales together at Christmas, are the most important gifts of all. "Giving and receiving of time, sharing in the making of memories, sharing life, these are the gifts that give you strong roots to grow," Yumi would say. Mary Iris ate one of Emily's cookies. It was good, but she thought that the ones from her mother's recipe were much better. Then she called Yumi to let her know what had happened and where she was. Yumi was glad she was safe, but was curious as to how Mary Iris was going to continue her trip. Mary Iris told Yumi that she would figure it out tomorrow, after a good night's sleep.

Mary Iris was tired from the long day and decided to go upstairs to go to bed.   As she lay down under the warm cozy covers, she looked out the window and saw a star.   She made a wish that she would arrive safely at her destination by Christmas Eve.

As it turned out, Chris was also making a wish to be home by Christmas.   He'd always been at home with his grandma. He felt bad about not being there, but was grateful that his grandma's friend was there with her.   At least she wasn't alone.   If all went well he would be leaving in two days and hopefully be home by Christmas Eve.

I'm only a small part of making these wishes come true.   The universe works together in these things… I tell you, it's simple and complicated all at the same time.   Sometimes you just never know what's gonna happen.

CHAPTER 10

WUJA

The next morning Mary Iris woke to the singing of a cardinal.   As she opened her eyes, she saw the bright red bird sitting on the windowsill. He was looking in as if to get her attention.

"Good morning little bird," she said to the cardinal as she tapped on the glass.

"Wuja,   Wuja,   Wuja,   Wuja,   open   the window?" the little bird asked.

Mary Iris opened the window and the little bird told Mary Iris his story.   He told her that his name was Wuja and that he had flown with his friend Robin south for the winter.   Once he gotten down south, he realized how much he missed his family.

"I'm headed *septentrional,"* he said.

"What's *septentrional?"* Mary Iris asked.

"North" he said.

"As a matter of fact I just happen to be heading septentrional myself!   Wherever did you learn such a word?"

"My parents taught me.   They teach me all sorts of things!" Wuja said pridefully as he ruffled his feathers. "Wuja take me with you?"

"Sure. It would be nice to have some company. Let me pack my things and I'll meet you on the front lawn."

As Mary Iris started down the stairs, she remembered what Yumi had taught her about animals that show up in your life and how they have special meanings. *Kind of like a secret message.*   She remembered that cardinals meant that there would be a return to joy. Mary Iris could hear Yumi clearly in her head.   *"When a cardinal enters your life, they help you to fulfill your dreams and help you to find you own song."*   Mary Iris now added meeting Wuja to her now extremely long list of miracles.

Mary Iris and Wuja headed into town stopping at the bakery to thank Emily for having a place to sleep.   She introduced Wuja to Emily.   "Wuja give us something to eat?" Wuja asked.   This embarrassed Mary Iris, but Emily laughed it off and gave the two of them some fresh gingerbread muffins and some hot chocolate.   The two thanked Emily once again and went outside to enjoy their breakfast as they watched the festivities starting to take place.

The town was all abuzz, and the life-sized gingerbread of Santa and his reindeer were all set and awaiting Santa's arrival.   The judges were looking at the entries of gingerbread houses that had been entered for the contest.   The chorus was getting ready to sing as excitement and joy filled the air. The only thing that Mary Iris could think about however, was spending Christmas with Yumi.

After finishing their breakfast, Mary Iris and Wuja went back into the bakery to thank Emily once again wishing each other a very Merry Christmas. As Mary Iris and Wuja left the bakery, she noticed a man sitting on a bench and asked him if he knew the best way to get up north would be.

"Water," he said pointing to the east. "Water will take you anywhere; it can even take you home. There's a boat dock down the road.   You can probably catch a ride on a boat that will take you up the coast."

Mary Iris thanked the man as she and Wuja started heading east.   Upon their arrival at the dock, they saw an old man fishing.   Mary Iris, being her naturally friendly self, asked the man if he had caught any fish and he replied by saying. "*One small fish and a lot of joy!*"

"What a lovely thought," she replied.   "Most people think the more fish you can catch the better. But what can be better than catching joy?"   This made her smile, not just on the outside, but gave her that warm fuzzy feeling on the inside too, the kind that makes your whole body smile.   "I hope you have a Merry Christmas," she said to the man as she and Wuja continued.

"Merry Christmas to you my friends, and May your heart be light!" he replied.

I noticed that since I had arrived, the Naysayer Cosmic Force was breaking away from Mary Iris little by little.   I felt that her heart was light, not the heavy heart I felt in her the past few years.

Soon after the encounter with the old man, Mary Iris saw a small unusual looking ship named, *The Alpha Centauri.* She saw people getting on and hoped there would be room for her and Wuja. As she approached the ships' landing, she saw the captain of the ship. "Where are you headed," she asked the captain?

"Tomorrow. We're headed for tomorrow, and yes, Mary Iris there is a spot just for you," the captain said with a smile on his face.

Mary Iris was puzzled. "How did you know my name?"

"A little bird told me," the captain answered as he winked at Wuja.

It was then that Mary Iris knew – no, she believed – that she was exactly where she needed to be.

I couldn't have choreographed it any better. I was on The Alpha Centauri and the Captain of the ship was none other than my star friend, Kapteyn. I thanked him for helping out. You are not going to believe what happened next!

CHAPTER 11

WISH IT – DREAM IT – DO IT

As Mary Iris boarded the ship, she introduced Wuja and herself to her shipmates. The passengers took turns telling their stories of where they were headed and how they came to this ship. They all seemed to be amazed at the single thread that held them together – like how they all had been stuck in some sort of a rut – but knew that this ship would get them out of it and where they needed to be.

Mary Iris confided to her shipmates that Yumi had taught her to believe in her wishes and dreams, and that life works with you if you just trust and believe in yourself. "I haven't believed that for a long time," she said, but continued by saying, "I'm starting to believe she was right."

I could see that the Naysayer Cosmic Force no longer had control over Mary Iris. I was not yet convinced however about the other passengers. Kapteyn and I were feeling on top of the world knowing what was about to take place. As only Kapteyn could do, he ordered that the sails be lifted.

These were no ordinary sails, they were *solar sails,* and within an instant, the sails were up, and off we went, no longer sailing the sea, but sailing the wind… starbound.!   The view was magnificent and I could see my friends like Sirius, Wolf 359, and Canopus. I even saw my star friend who didn't have a name. Needless to say, the passengers were amazed by what was happening.   Kapteyn, clapping his hands to get everyone's attention, announced that it was time for class.   Everyone looked puzzled even though I knew what was about to take place.

"Class on what… how to sail this ship?" one passenger asked.

"Class about stars?" asked another.

"No," replied Kapteyn.   "I am a professor of *Wish Theory.*   You will be learning the art of wishing properly."

This caught everyone's attention and they all followed Kapteyn to the area of the deck that was set-up with benches and a lectern.   Posed at the lectern, Kapteyn started by saying; "You have all been carefully chosen to be here at this time and this place. It is important for you to know that *wishing* should never be for selfish reasons."   As he said this he pointed to a passenger named Thaddeus, a man maybe in his thirties, who was there with his father Robert and his son Derek.

Thaddeus caught off-guard said, "I don't think I make selfish wishes."

"Of course you don't Thaddeus," Kapteyn said, "But, your father and your son have."   To this statement, Thaddeus looked confused.

"Robert, what did you wish for Thaddeus when he was growing up?" Kapteyn asked.

"I wished that Thaddeus would grow up to be a banker like me, like my father was, and his father was," said Robert.

"Exactly," Kapteyn said sternly. "And tell me, Thaddeus, are you a banker?"

"No, I'm a waste engineer."

"He's a garbage man," Derek piped up.

Then Kapteyn looked at Derek and asked, "So, what is your wish young man?"

"I wished my dad wasn't a garbage man. It's embarrassing."

"So, Thaddeus," continued Kapteyn, "tell me... do you ... forgive me if I say... like being a garbage man?"

Thaddeus told Kapteyn and everyone else on the ship exactly how he felt. "I chose to be a garbage man." He explained; "I like to be outside, I like the people on my route, I like to help keep the town free of debris, I like to think that I make a difference on what actually is *garbage* and what can be put to other uses. But, most of all I like that I'm home by the time Derek gets home from school. I'm able to help him with his homework, we play ball, and go for bike rides together. I know my dad loves me," Thaddeus said as he put his arms around his dad, "but dad worked long hours at the bank and spending time with him was something that I missed from my childhood. I didn't want that for Derek."

Kapteyn pointed out, that maybe the proper wish for Robert, would have been, *I wish for my son to enjoy his work and live a full and happy life.* With tears in his eyes, Robert agreed.   He admitted that he never really wanted to be a banker, but became one because his father wanted him to.   Robert was proud that Thaddeus had the courage to follow his heart and Derek was no longer embarrassed that his dad was a *garbage* man.   He realized how much he enjoys spending time with his dad when he gets home from school, and couldn't imagine it any other way. Derek now understood that it isn't one's job that makes a person, it's how the person himself *feels* about what he or she is doing.

Then, there was Wendell and his twin sister Wendy.   Things came easy for Wendy, but not so much for Wendell.   The one thing Wendell had to his advantage was humor and that… was why *they* were on the *Alpha Centauri.*   The two were on their way to the university where Wendell was to attend.   It was a special university.   You see Wendell could not hear or see.   Since we stars can speak all languages, Kapteyn spoke to Wendell in a way he understood. It's called *tactile signing.*

"Do you have a wish?" Kapteyn signed to Wendell.

"Of course I do…"   he signed back to Kapteyn, as he took a deep breath and paused, "I wish that I could be a…"   he continued signing slowly almost as if he was afraid to reveal his wish, "C-L-O-W-N."

Kapteyn told us what his wish was.   Well, I can only say we never imagined that would be his wish.   We thought it might be that he wished he could see or hear, but be a *clown,* never.

Wendell told Kapteyn in his language, that when he and his sister were ten years old, the family went to the circus. "Even though I could not see or hear, I could feel the happiness from the clowns. One of the clowns came into the audience, right up to me... I learned from him for the first time, how to be silly.   Wendy was afraid of the clown, and I thought... How could that be?   Sometimes I think that people who can see, well, I think they sometimes are blinder than I am," Wendell signed to Kapteyn and smiled.   "I hope that I can teach people, that the way a person makes you *feel* is what is most important.   That's why I wish to be a clown."

Kapteyn thought that was a wonderful idea. He actually knew of a clown school close to the university where Wendell was going to attend.   He said he'd make sure that Wendell got enrolled there. Wendell put out his hand to shake Kapteyn's hand. As Kapteyn reached out for Wendell's, Wendell could sense he was getting close and pulled his hand away.   Everybody laughed when all of a sudden there was a loud "baaaaa."

"Well, well, well, what do we have here?" Kapteyn said as he walked over to a crate which was where the sound was coming from. There was a note on the crate that read:

Dear Sir,

I have heard about you being an expert on wishes and thought maybe you could help. My name is Colin. I'm 12 years old and live on a farm. "Galileo" was born last spring and as you can see he is purple. I have a way with animals. They speak to me in a way that I understand. Galileo told me he wants to be a "seeing eye sheep." I'm wishing that you can make it so.

Thank you sir, and Merry Christmas,

Colin

"Timing is everything," Kapteyn said as he and Galileo walked over to Wendell to convey what had just happened. He asked Wendell if he would like Galileo as his seeing-eye sheep. Wendell smiled and shook his head up and down as Kapteyn took Wendell's hand and placed it on Galileo's soft wool. Wendell wrapped his arms around him and Galileo gave a very happy "baaaa."

Everyone could see that Wendell and Galileo made the perfect pair and I noticed that tears of joy were streaming down everyone's cheeks. This made me wonder…. How does it happen that one can cry both when they are happy and sad????

Next, Kapteyn talked about stars and proper motion and how wishes have their own proper motion. He said, "First, you must **Wish** it, and wish it from your heart, not your head. If it feels good in your heart…

go ahead and make your wish.   Next, *Dream* it!
Imagine what your wish will look like when it comes
true.   And, last but not least, *Do* it!   Don't just
expect that your wish will come true without any
effort on your part.   We stars can't do all the work.
Why if we did, we wouldn't have enough energy to
shine.   Take a necessary step or action towards what
you wish and we'll help you along the way.   Then,
take another step... and then, when the time is right,
and everything is in its *proper motion...* that *wish*,
will come true!

     Kapteyn   warned   everybody   about   the
Naysayer Cosmic Force.   He told them, "They look
like stars, but don't let them fool you, they're
imposters.   They're just waiting for the wrong kinds
of wishes to come their way and turn those people
into *Naysayers.* Then, the people who have become
Naysayers, well, they contaminate innocent people
with their negative energy.   If you come in contact
with one... all I can say is... Protect Your Wish!"

     The class continued as other passengers also
shared in their wishes. Jaja wished to go back to
Africa to rebuild his family's cocoa plantation. Zaylee
wished to become a doctor so she could help her
sister who was sick.   Then Kapteyn answered any
last questions to close out the class.

     Mary Iris was listening very closely to
everything Kapteyn said and tried to think back on
some of her wishes.   She remembered the special
wish that she had made as a child, the one that I was
now there to help make come true.   Then she thought
about the one just the night before, the one to get to

her destination safely by Christmas.   Shifting her thoughts to the present, she wondered where Wuja was.   She asked around to see if anybody had seen him.   Kapteyn told her that there was a room down below that had a perfect spot for Wuja to perch himself on and he believed that he might be there. Mary Iris thanked Kapteyn for everything and left to go check to see if she could find her feathered friend.

This was my chance. Since I wanted to meet Mary Iris face to face and knew that she would not be able to see me as a star, I changed myself into looking like a passenger of the *Alpha Centauri.*   Earlier in the evening, I sent a message to some of my musical star friends, asking them for help.   When I saw Mary Iris go to check on Wuja, I gave my star friends the cue and they responded note by note by playing the beautiful song from Mary Iris' music box.   She couldn't believe what she was hearing, and she began to dance.   I watched her every move. I knew this might be the only chance I would ever get to meet her face to face.   I held out my hand and we danced. For that brief time I thought that I would never want to be a star again.   As the music faded I said; "Goodnight Binah.   Your wishes will come true,"   and I kissed her softly on her cheek.   She put her hand on her cheek where I had kissed her, wondering how I knew her as *Binah.*

All of a sudden, the Alpha Centauri warning alarm went off.   Kapteyn warned everyone that up ahead was a strong Naysayer Cosmic Force.   He gave everyone the option to safely go around it, which would mean an extra day of travel… or stick together and try to confuse it and land at our original scheduled time.   Hopefully nobody would be turned into a Naysayer in the process.   We all decided that if we stuck together, we could get back on track.

Luckily for us, our star friends that were nearby could see what was happening and they gave us the most spectacular show that anyone would ever want to see.   The Naysayer Cosmic Force didn't have a chance with all their antics.   We sailed through safely, leaving only stardust behind.   All the excitement from what had taken place since we first set sail made us all a little weary and felt it was time to turn in.   We would dream our dreams and then… it would be *tomorrow.*

Kapteyn is very wise and I realize that I'm lucky to have him not only as my friend, but as my mentor.

CHAPTER 12

NEW YORK

The Alpha Centauri landed back in the waters the next morning and by that afternoon we had docked in New York City. As we all got off the ship, everyone said their good-byes and continued on, feeling grateful for the lessons they had learned. I noticed that everyone had a little more spring in their step and I was grateful to Kapteyn for this.

Off in the distance, Mary Iris heard singing and decided to travel towards the beautiful sound with Wuja perched on her shoulder. I of course followed along. As we approached the merriment of song and dance, we saw the most beautiful Christmas tree, all lit up with colorful lights. And Wuja... well, wouldn't you know it, he had found his family. There they were looking like ornaments; dozens of his cardinal family had joined together at Rockefeller Center to adorn the famous tree. Wuja thanked Mary Iris for helping him to make this happen and joyously flew off to be with his family.

Mary Iris stood there taking in the sights and sounds of the season. The dancers seemed to be both of the professional sort and those who just couldn't help but be part of this celebration. There were musicians and instruments of all kinds, trumpets, cellos, guitars, even pails that were turned upside down and used as drums. Those without instruments were clapping their hands in time with the music. The people were diverse as well... young, old, rich, poor, seemingly from all parts of the world, some with families and some by themselves. It was a beautiful sight, all joining in the universal language of song and dance to celebrate "Peace on Earth" in the Spirit of Christmas.

There was a child who told the story of Hanukkah and how it's the *Festival of Light.* Then the music got quite lively again and everyone joined in singing and dancing to *Auld Lang Syne* as it was sung in different languages. When it was over, a meal was offered to anyone who was hungry. Mary Iris decided that it was time for her to continue on. As she was leaving she heard; "Merry Christmas, Feliz Navidad, Joeux Noel, God Jul, Buon Natale, and Happy Hanukkah." She felt this was a sign that maybe her wish was starting to come true.

I'm telling you, the light that shined from all the people gathered that night was brighter than any of us stars ever could be.

Wuja noticed Mary Iris leaving and flew back to thank his new friend for being so kind. He hoped that someday their paths might cross again. It was at that moment when it started to snow. Mary Iris couldn't believe her eyes. It was the most beautiful sight she had ever seen.   It was so white, coming down looking like shimmering crystals. As she stood there in awe and marveled at this ordinary miracle, she couldn't help but think that the snowflakes felt like tiny little kisses as they touched her cheeks. Then, she remembered seeing once in a movie someone sticking his tongue out to catch snowflakes. So that was what she did. ˙ I saw the first one that landed on her tongue and it made her smile. Not only with her mouth, but with her whole face!

The snow was falling steadily as Mary Iris started walking, thinking of what she was going to do next. She thought maybe a she could take a bus. Out of the corner of her eye, she caught a glimpse of a pay phone.   She remembered Yumi telling her about pay phones and she ran to it thinking she could call her to let her know where she was and ask her advice.   Not realizing just how slippery the snow was, her feet came out from underneath her and she fell to the ground.   Looking up at the snow falling down she saw a glimmer of light thinking maybe she was seeing stars.

"I wish someone could help me," she said.

Well, it was me that she saw, or should I say the twinkling of me. And... how was I going to deny her another wish? I had to think fast!

CHAPTER 13

THE STARLIGHT LOUNGE

Across the street from where Mary Iris had taken her fall, I noticed a building called, *The Starlight Lounge.* Who did I see there? It was none other than my friend, Kapteyn, sipping on a warm drink.   I knew Kapteyn had already done everything he could do, he was kind of like what you might say… *off the clock.* But, I thought surely someone inside would help. So, in all my *wizardness*, I turned myself into a boy and ran into the lounge.   Out of breath, I told the bartender that there was a girl across the street that was looking to get to Coventry, Connecticut tonight and asked if he or anyone here could help her.

The bartender asked around, but everybody seemed too busy feeling sorry for themselves because they had no other place to go on a night when most people are celebrating with their families. To them, the lounge had become their home and their family, even though they didn't seem to realize it.   Kapteyn just shook his head.   He could see that they were family.   They were different than Naysayer's.   They were what we call, *The Forgotten.   Forgottens'* don't remember what it's like to feel happy, to care, or… feel cared about.   Kapteyn noticed all of this going on and felt confident that things were about to change for the better.

I begged with the bartender that he had to do something.   Surely he knew someone who could help.   He told me that he might know someone and went to make a phone call.   As I watched him talking on the phone with his head nodding and a smile starting to form, he gave me a *thumbs up*.   He poured two hot apple ciders, gave one to me, and the other he brought outside to Mary Iris.   I followed him leaving my cider by the door, and listened as he told her that she would have a ride soon and should be in Coventry, Connecticut before midnight.   As he turned around to talk to me, I was nothing but a glimmer of light and a warm feeling in his heart.   He stayed with Mary Iris until she was picked up by a yellow car that said *Taxi* on it and told the driver to take her to the airport.

You know, something did happen inside the lounge as all of that was going on.   The people watched as the bartender helped Mary Iris.   They witnessed one person helping another, and somehow… like magic, they realized that they were grateful for each other, the bartender, and The Starlight Lounge.   They *had* become family.   And tonight, this was their home.   They started sharing stories about Christmas' past, knowing that this moment too would bring them fond memories.   They were smiling, and off in the corner, Kapteyn was smiling too!

I was but stardust at this point affixing myself to the roof of that taxi, holding on for dear life, but yet very much enjoying the ride!

CHAPTER 14

THE BLUE EAGLE

As the taxi approached the airport, Mary Iris looked at the instructions the bartender had given her.   It said…

Go to the last terminal and you'll see a plane called "The Blue Eagle."   The pilot should be there waiting for you.   He'll fly you to your destination.
Wishing you a Merry Christmas!

Winston

Stepping out of the taxi, Mary Iris held the instructions close to her chest, looked up at the night sky and said; "Thank you Winston, and Merry Christmas to you too!"   The anticipation was making her heart beat fast. She walked through the corridor of the terminal thinking about everything that had happened and all the people she met in such a short time. She couldn't wait to tell Yumi and was looking forward to finally meeting Coralee. There it was, *The Blue Eagle,* a small plane and Mary Iris wondered if the person looking out the window was the pilot.   He was dressed in jeans and a sweater and she didn't think he looked old enough to be a pilot.   But she shrugged her shoulders and thought; *"Well, this can't be so bad. After all I did get on the Alpha Centauri."*

She approached the young man and asked him if he knew where the pilot for the Blue Eagle was. After he told her that he was the pilot, she introduced herself and the two boarded the plane.

Oh, my, my, my... was I ever surprised!

"I really appreciate what you are doing for me since its Christmas and all," Mary Iris said as she buckled herself into the seat.

"No problem," the pilot replied.   "I was headed up to Coventry anyway when I got the message over the radio that Winston needed a favor."

The pilot told her to hang tight since it was still snowing and might be a tricky takeoff.   It wasn't too bad considering, and being the star that I am, I followed.   As they reached cruising altitude, the pilot asked Mary Iris if she had ever been to Coventry before.   She told him it was her first time.   "I'm going spend Christmas with Yumi who's like a mother to me and her friend Coralee Turner. Coralee's the one who lives in Coventry.   Do you know her?"

"Well, actually, yes I do.   Coralee is my Grandma.   She told me there was going to be a girl joining us, but she said her name was Binah.   Oh, and by the way, I don't think I've properly introduced myself.   I'm Chris Turner." Mary Iris smiled and explained that Yumi gave her the nickname of Binah because it means, one who dances and told Chris how she loves to dance.

"Maybe you can teach me sometime," Chris said hoping that she would.

"With pleasure," Mary Iris answered as she felt her face blushing.

They were now flying above the cloud cover and could see all the stars. Mary Iris told Chris about Shambahla, which is why she decided to come to Coventry. She also told him about all that had happened on her journey, like meeting Emily Johnson and Wuja. She told him about Kapteyn and the Alpha Centauri with its solar sail, the passengers and learning about proper wishes. She continued telling Chris about the Naysayer's and how they try to put a kibosh on wishes, and then finally ending up at Rockefeller Center. After that she met Winston who put her in the taxi with the note, which brought her to this moment.

"Wow, that's an amazing story," Chris said, not really sure if he should believe it.

"It's not a story Chris," Mary Iris stated with conviction. "I'm not sure that I'd even believe it if I hadn't experienced it myself. But, as sure as I am sitting right here... It's the truth!"

Then it was Chris' turn. He told Mary Iris that he helps people who have been affected by natural disasters. He told her that he had hoped to be in Coventry a couple of days ago, but was delayed to make sure the last family got into their home for Christmas. "If I hadn't been delayed, we probably wouldn't be taking this flight right now," Chris said.

"Yumi would have been home for Christmas, which means you wouldn't have taken this journey."

I could tell by the look on both of their faces that they seemed content in how everything came to this particular moment in time.   And for me... I was more than content. I was on cloud nine, over the moon... oh, you know what I mean, ECSTATIC. My two wishers, the ones I travelled here to Earth for, to make sure their wishes would come true, were now sitting side by side.   My mission would soon be complete!

CHAPTER 15

TOGETHER AT LAST

Chris landed safely at Mr. Avery's Airport and the two hopped on the trolley which brought them to Main Street in Coventry. The town was all aglow with lights and the windows of the stores were decorated for Christmas. The blanket of snow reflected the lights making it look like a bed of crystals, and even though the air was cold, it had a gentleness about it. As Mary Iris and Chris stepped off the trolley, they walked arm in arm. It would be just a few short blocks to his grandma's house. Chris was relieved to be almost home and Mary Iris' eyes were open wide with amazement by the sights that she was taking in. To her, the town looked like something that she had only seen in pictures before.

The town was filled with people who had just finished attending the candlelight church service. They noticed Chris and welcomed him back to Coventry wishing him a Merry Christmas, knowing that his grandma was anxiously awaiting his arrival. Chris introduced Mary Iris as Binah to everyone, since they knew that a girl named Binah would be joining the Turner family for Christmas. It was quite the homecoming!

Coralee's house was a two story with a front porch just like Mary Iris imagined. There was a Christmas tree in the large picture window with its lights on. As the two walked up the steps to the front door, Yumi opened it to greet them. "Mi pequeña Binah, i estás aquí! Hola, Chris, feliz navidad. Oh, forgive me, I'm so excited to see both of you, come in," Yumi said in all the excitement. She wrapped her arms around both of them as they headed inside. Chris went over to Coralee who was sitting on the sofa by the fireplace and gave her a kiss on the cheek and sat down beside her. Yumi introduced Mary Iris as Binah as they sat on the chairs across from the sofa.

Mary Iris and Chris told Yumi and Coralee how they came to meet each other. Mary Iris told the story of everything that had happened to her on her journey and all the people that she had met. As she finished telling her story, the clock in the hall chimed that it was midnight. Yumi and Mary Iris looked at each other and let out a... "Cock-a-doodle-doo." Yumi then told her story of the Misa de Gallo in Guatemala and how there are fireworks to celebrate Christmas. As everyone was listening to Yumi, Chris leaned over to Mary Iris and whispered something in her ear and then politely excused himself.

Mary Iris asked if she might be able to have a cup of tea, so all the ladies went into the kitchen. They were sitting around the kitchen table that looked out into the back yard. Even though it was dark outside, the white of the snow could be seen. All of a sudden there was a loud boom and a flash of beautiful colors filled the sky.   Chris had gone out to the shed where he had some leftover fireworks from the fourth of July.   One after another, blue, red, green and bright white ones that looked like shimmering stars.   Yumi was over struck with joy as it was the first time since she came to America that she saw fireworks on Christmas.   After the fireworks show was over, Mary Iris, Yumi, and Coralee clapped as they watched Chris take a bow.   Then with his arms in the air he fell backwards and made a snow angel.

When Chris came back inside, they all had one more cup of Coralee's special Christmas tea as they talked about how beautiful the fireworks were with the snow on the ground and how this might just be the start of a new tradition.   It was getting late and time to say goodnight.   They all agreed that they would continue their Christmas celebration in the morning.

Yumi came into Mary Iris' bedroom to say goodnight and tell her how happy she was that they arrived safely.   Mary Iris told Yumi that through everything that happened, she felt more confident in herself, like this experience was some sort of a test. "Learning about wishes and the Naysayer Cosmic Force from Kapteyn made me realize that I had given up on myself and my dreams.   The song from the music box you gave me played while I was on the Alpha Centauri and I danced.   Then, when I was in New York and saw people from all over the world singing and dancing to celebrate what you taught me so many years ago, *that this is the time of year we celebrate the light that we all have inside us to share with the world.*   Well, I knew that I still wanted to study how and why people dance.   It truly is a universal language.   But even more, I want to teach people how important it is to believe in themselves." With that Mary Iris gave a big yawn and said good-night to Yumi.

"Oh, Binah," Yumi said as she kissed her forehead, "your wish will come true just as mine has."

It was quite the homecoming. Now… I just needed to wait for Santa.

CHAPTER 16

SANTA'S ARRIVAL

While everyone was sleeping, I waited for Santa. I was a little nervous because I have seen just how busy he is on Christmas Eve from where I live and was hoping that he would be able to take time out to talk to me.   I knew that I didn't have to change myself into a human form for him to see me.   As I waited patiently looking up at the sky, which had now cleared, I could see my friends in all their proper places.   I even saw that little star that had helped me out more than once.   Then, in a flash I saw Santa coming in for his landing.   He noticed me right away.

As he got out of his sleigh, I went over to greet him.   I told him how honored I was to meet him in person as I have been watching the work that he does for years and years.   I introduced myself and told him that I was from the Galaxy of Dreamers, here to make sure that Mary Iris' wish was granted and I couldn't do it without him.   I told him it was a heart wish.

"Ahhh, a heart wish," Santa said stroking his beard. "I'm familiar with those.   I once in my off season went for a ride with Kapteyn on the Alpha Centauri.   He taught me all about heart wishes and how you stars work your magic to help them come true. You see, I get a lot of Christmas wishes, most of which come from children who want a certain toy. Those are easy. Every so often I do get a heart wish, which of course warms my heart, but they are more challenging to grant. Kapteyn helped me tremendously with how those wishes get granted."

"Well," I said, "Eleven years ago Mary Iris wished to spread happiness while teaching dances from around the world. I know you have helped her by the books and music you have given her and I thank you for that. But, she needed more and I was destined to help her make sure that her wish would come true. When I landed here a couple of days ago, I helped her on her journey to believe in herself again. She will go on to teach others to believe in themselves and the world will be a happier place because of it."

"Wonderful," said Santa, "We need more people like Mary Iris in this world. I'm glad you were able to help make her wish come true. Merry Christmas Will, now if you'll excuse me I must continue my work. I have a lot to finish before the break of day."

"Wait, there's one more thing. Something that I need your help with, that only you can do. Mary Iris also wished that very same night, that she could be on your Magic List just as Yulianna is. I was wondering perhaps, if there was any way you might consider that part of her wish to come true?"

Right then and there, he did it! Oh twinkle dee dee; Mary Iris' wish would be fulfilled. The certificate read;

*This certificate is awarded to Mary
Iris/Binah
as an honorary member of Santa's
Magic List.*
Signed;   *Santa Claus*

I loved this Christmas thing here on Earth and I too had a present for Mary Iris.   I asked Santa if he would be so kind as to put it under the Christmas tree with the rest of the presents.   He told me that he most definitely would.   I thanked him and wished him a Merry Christmas.   He thanked me for helping to make heart wishes come true.

I watched through the window as Santa carefully lay all the presents under the tree, including the certificate for Mary Iris and the present from me. Then in a flash, as quickly as he arrived, he left, waving good-bye wishing me a Merry Christmas.

My work was almost finished.   Being my magical self, I entered Chris' dream that night.   He dreamt about the night he wished on me and he could see all the events that had lead up to this evening and on to the future.   After leaving his dream, I figured I might as well stick around for a little while longer to experience up close what Christmas morning was really like here on Earth.   Of course, as proper motion would have it, the yellow dwarf star known as *The Sun,* started shining brightly in all her glory, which woke everybody up.

I can't tell you how happy I was,
that I was here on Earth
to witness Christmas morning.

CHAPTER 17

CHRISTMAS MORNING

Coralee started by asking Chris if he would pass out the presents.   The first one he chose was to Coralee from Yumi.   It was a beautiful *huipil* that Yumi had made herself.   Next was a present to Mary Iris from Chris.   She seemed surprised since they had just met last night and apologized for not having a gift for him, but Chris didn't mind.   Inside the box was a picture of Yumi, Coralee, and Mary Iris sitting around the kitchen table while the fireworks were going off. You could see the reflection of the fireworks from the glass with all three of the expressions on their faces looking like they were saying; *"oooooooohhhhh."* "Thank you Chris, it's beautiful!" she said as she passed it on for Yumi and Coralee to look at.

Yumi got her usual fruits and candies from Santa and Chris got some new tools to help him with his work.   Next, this was it. The fulfillment of Mary Iris' wish from Santa…. As she held it in her hands, she guessed it was a book because she usually gets a book from Santa. She was excited because she knows that he picks the best ones just for her.   Well, she could hardly believe her eyes.   "Yumi," she said with amazement, "Look, I made it!   Just like you, I made it!   I am now an honorary member of Santa's Magic List."   Yumi was bursting with joy. And for me... I felt a sense of pride witnessing this event.

The rest of the gifts were passed out and opened.   As all the wrapping was being gathered, Chris noticed one more present towards the back of the tree.   It said; *To Binah.*   Mary Iris looked puzzled as he handed it to her since she had already received a present from everyone and the handwriting was one she didn't recognize.   She opened the envelope first and read the letter...

Dear Binah,

My name is Will; I am a Star... from the Galaxy of Dreamers.   There's an ancient legend that says each star carries the soul of one person.   I am lucky to carry you.   Usually we stars just watch over our soul mates, and I have watched you since you were born.   But as it happened, in a one in a trillion chance, one night many years ago, you made a wish on me.   Not only you, but also Chris.   This sent me on my journey to Earth.   I arrived a few days ago and have been with you on your journey to Coventry every step of the way.

As a star, you can only see me in the night sky, but here on Earth, I can change myself to look like a human for a short time.   You might remember me.   I was the man who told you; "Water can take you anywhere," and I was the one you danced with on The Alpha Centauri, as I said to you; "Good night Binah, your wishes will come true," as I kissed you gently on the cheek.   You see, Kapteyn is my friend. He helped me arrange that you would take that ride. I loved how you told everyone that they must believe in magic.   The world needs people like you.   I was also that little boy who went into the Starlight Lounge when I saw that you needed some help getting to Coventry.   It was a miracle, (another one you can add to your list), that it was Chris who was your pilot. Even I was surprised!

I have learned much from watching you and Yumi.... Unconditional love, joy and sorrow, how to make a friend, and ... caring. And, through that caring, I've noticed how you help people to believe in themselves, even though for a time you questioned it yourself.

On this journey, I met a little star who helped me through some difficult times. She didn't have a name and still continued to help. She has the same kind of spirit I see in you. I talked to Kapteyn about her and she now has officially been given a name. She was named after you and Yumi, for all the light that we see because of you. The little stars name is BiYu. I took the Bi from Binah and the Yu from Yumi to come up with it. Yumi gave me the idea of combining names when you were just a baby. BiYu stands for..."Believe in Your uniqueness." And, as you know, we are all unique.

I watched that little star in the sky last night when she received her name and I actually think she shined a little brighter because of it. She's looking forward to the day she too gets wished on. She lives in Ursa Major, otherwise known as; "The Big Dipper," towards the bottom left side. You'll have to look closely as there are others that are brighter than her, but none that I can think of that have a brighter spirit.

Thank you for your wishes, as they help to make us stars live our purpose. Keep dancing, and teach people how to wish properly and believe in themselves.   Also, tell Chris that in time the rest of his wish will come true!

With love, your shining star,

Will

Mary Iris folded the letter and put it back in the envelope.   Then she opened the box.   Inside was a necklace with a star inscribed with "BiYu."   She put it on and read the note I put inside the box;

This star is a reminder that I will always be with you.   Even when you can't see me, I am still there.   Believe in Your uniqueness, and I will see your light shine just as you see mine.
Merry Christmas, Will

Mary Iris walked over to Chris and told him that in time the rest of his wish will come true.   They continued their Christmas celebration with Yumi announcing she had one more surprise for everyone.

"To the kitchen," she said clapping her hands. And, there on the counter were all the ingredients to make the gingerbread cookies.   "Now you didn't think we were going to go without making gingerbread cookies did you?"   Everyone chipped in making the cookies in different shapes. They even made stars, writing "Will" on one, and "BiYu" on another.

With that, I started heading back home.

CHAPTER 18

HOME AGAIN

Off I was, heading back home. I continued to watch Mary Iris as I still do today. Yumi and Mary Iris went to Africa after the New Year. Mary Iris had told Yumi about Jaja wanting to rebuild his family's cocoa plantation and knew that Yumi would be able to help. It was a great experience as Yumi used her wisdom and knowledge of the theobroma trees to teach Jaja all the secrets from her Mayan heritage. Mary Iris helped out at a local school teaching the children how to read. They in turn taught her the local dances. At night they would look at the stars and she would tell the story of how to wish properly, just like she had learned from Kapteyn. They stayed for almost one year, and today the cocoa plantation is thriving. Jaja named a chocolate bar after Yumi called; *"The Yumi Chocolate Bar."*

After leaving Africa, they went to Guatemala for a visit with Yumi's parents. Yumi's papi played his homemade marimba and they all enjoyed singing and dancing to his songs. Yumi's mami whom Mary Iris called *abuelita,* told Mary Iris stories of when Yumi was a young girl in Guatemala and how happy she was that Coralee had chosen her to go to the

University.   "Al que nace para tamal, de cielo le caen las hojas," she said to Mary Iris.   Mary Iris looked at Yumi knowing that what she said means; *If you're born to be a tamale, corn husks will fall from the sky.* The two just smiled knowing that what she meant was… your destiny will find you.   I personally like to think of it as; *The universe always has a plan and it is written in the stars!*

Mary Iris and Chris continued to see each other when possible and Mary Iris even went with Chris one time to help a community that had been hit with an earthquake.   That year when they went back to Coventry at Christmas, they told Yumi and Coralee they were getting married.   It took a while, but at long last, the rest of Chris' wish came true.   Just in case you don't remember, Chris wanted a family of his own someday.

As the years went by, they had their family. Three daughters… Patience, Honor, and Chloe Esta. They're a beautiful, loving, caring family who were brought up to believe in their uniqueness.   Patience now lives in California and is an olive farmer and a teacher.   She teaches math, health, and social studies by way of the olive.   Quite unique I must say. Patience is married and has a son named William Yule.   *I like to think that Mary Iris had something to do with naming him. After me perhaps?*   Honor is a principal of a school.   She sees that the teachers inspire to teach the children not only to succeed academically, but more importantly to succeed in the human spirit as well.   And Chloe Esta, well, she is an astronomer who is currently working on making sure *The Galaxy of Dreamers,* becomes officially named along with the other galaxies. She has a dog named Sirius.

Each year at Christmas, the family gathers in Coventry Connecticut to continue their family traditions.   Yumi pulls out the gingerbread cookie recipe as they share stories of the past, present, and wishes for the future while making the cookies.   On Christmas Eve, Coralee makes the tea, as Chris goes outside for the annual Christmas fireworks display. Then they all go outside and look up in the sky for BiYu and me.   They make their official Christmas wishes and we give a little twinkle back to them to let them know we received their wish.   It is then that I work my magic and the snow starts to fall.   Joy fills the air and their hearts… and we stars are happy to make heart wishes come true.   And because of all of this, the earth has been shining brighter.

When I travelled back home so many years ago, as I noticed *BiYu* waiting patiently for a wish to come her way, I thought I might just try myself to make a wish on her.   So I did!   My wish was that everyone would know this story.   So tell me… now do you believe in wishes??? Go ahead give it a try. Make a wish.   Make sure it's a heart wish, one that not only benefits you, but the rest of the world.   Then don't forget what Kapteyn taught…

Wish it… Dream it… Do it

The End

Unless,

of course you made a wish...

*T*hen it might just be

The Beginning!

The Family Gingerbread

Cookie Recipe

2 cups flour
½ teaspoon salt
½ teaspoon baking soda
1 teaspoon baking powder
1 teaspoon ginger
1 teaspoon cloves
1 ½ teaspoon cinnamon
½ teaspoon nutmeg
½ cup shortening
½ cup sugar
½ cup molasses
1 egg separated

In a mixing bowl, cream the shortening with the sugar and molasses until light and fluffy.   Beat in the egg yolk only. (Save the egg white in the refrigerator for later)   Mix in dry ingredients.   Make sure to add love and laughter and don't forget to take pictures.
    Preheat the oven to 350 degrees.

Roll out dough to about ¼ inch thickness and cut out with your favorite shapes.   Place on cookie sheet. Sometimes you may want to make two batches so you can trace your hands to make "hand cookies."   The last scraps of dough always get pressed into a circle. Bake for 8 – 10 minutes.   Cool on wire rack.

If one happens to break when you're taking them off the cookie sheet, I recommend eating it right away! Don't forget to share.

Icing
1 ½ cups powdered sugar   1/8 teaspoon cream of tartar   Reserved egg white
¼ teaspoon vanilla

Add all ingredients into medium bowl and mix at high speed until icing holds its shape.   Put icing in decorator tube (or plastic sandwich bag and cut off small corner).   Time to decorate and don't forget the sprinkles and hot cinnamon candies.

Continue with the love and laughter and don't forget to take more pictures.   A few cookies might disappear as they get decorated, this happens sometimes.   Hopefully you will have enough left to share for Christmas.

ACKNOWLEDGMENTS

First I would like to thank my wonderful family, all of you, even those who are here only in spirit. I love you all. To my friends, Denise, Lucia, and Patty, thank-you for your friendship and for being the first to listen to *Wish* in its entirety along with being so supportive of making my *Wish* come true. To Joanie, Vicki, and Marianne, I thank-you for your friendship and for listening to the story as well. Thank-you Susan for believing in the story enough to pass it on to Dick who passed it on to Kevin who gave *Wish* a wonderful review along with direction in the publishing process. Many thanks to you Kevin for that!

Thank you to my teacher and friend Luisa for expanding my knowledge and curiosity for Guatemala and its people. To Judy, I thank-you for the time you spent in the editing process, it is very much appreciated. To Jose, thank you for working your magic on the cover. To Andrea who gave me her beautiful necklace that said "Wish" on it hoping it would bring me good luck, your kindness will never be forgotten. To those who I have not mentioned by name, and have been involved in any way in my journey, I say thank-you.

ABOUT THE AUTHOR

Gail Wells was born in Chicago and raised in Rolling Meadows, Illinois. She currently resides in Woodstock, Illinois as do her grown children. Gail's many interests include being creative such as; dance, gardening, cooking, reading, writing, business, teaching, storytelling, music, and the human spirit. *Wish* is her first book.

Made in the USA
San Bernardino, CA
30 October 2015